CRY IN THE DARKNESS

A SHORT STORY

ALEXANDRIA BLAELOCK

BlueMere Books
MELBOURNE, AUSTRALIA

For permission requests, please contact
enquiries@bluemerebooks.com.

Ordering Information:
Discounts are available on quantity purchases. For details, contact orders@bluemerebooks.com.

Cry in the Darkness/Alexandria Blaelock
paperback ISBN: 978-1-922744-23-4
digital ISBN: 978-1-922744-24-1

CRY IN THE DARKNESS

The night was breathtakingly hot, close and still.

So dark Tom could barely see an inch in front of him.

The moon was hiding behind the clouds, but here and there a star pierced the gloom with unexpected brightness.

There's too much sky out here.

Trees stretched from horizon to horizon, like an invading army marching relentlessly forward in phalanx formation.

Tucked safely behind their shields, they had no regard for anyone in their way - if you didn't get out of it, they'd mow you down as if you were hay.

There were more creatures than people out here, and in the darkness, they rustled in the bushes.

Their quiet scurrying was an almost continuous assault on Tom's ears, terrifying because he didn't know what they were.

Or whether they ate people.

Or just killed them for fun, and left the remains for scavengers.

You came across half-eaten corpses of things all the time.

He sat on the trunk of a big old gum he'd felled himself with an axe.

It'd taken days, and he had the sore shoulders and blistered hands to prove it.

So torn and blistered he had to wrap them in rags to protect them from the heat of his tin cup and plate.

Even worse, he'd have to do it all again in the morning.

And the next day.

And the one after that.

Tom sighed and leant forward to poke the fire with a stick.

Sparks spattered and flew into the sky.

The oils and resin in the wood popped and flared.

Fires were supposed to be cheerful things.

But Tom had shrunk into himself with pain, fear and defeat. It seemed the surviving eucalypts were leaning menacingly in towards him.

As if they might snatch him up and tear him to pieces in retribution for their fallen comrades.

Fair enough, he supposed.

The pieces he'd stacked up nearby leaked resin. Red, like blood.

Staining the wood as it dripped down to the ground.

When they dried out and were trimmed down, they'd become the walls of his cottage.

Or maybe fence posts, which seemed a demeaning end for a majestic tree that had fought so valiantly to survive.

He was all alone, in wild bushland, with real and supernatural creatures he didn't understand and who didn't understand him.

Lord knows what possessed him to take passage to this inescapably God-forsaken land.

He'd thought there was a fortune to be made.

Though he hadn't reckoned on having to fight nature tooth and nail, day and night, in unrelenting back-breaking, soul-destroying labour.

He was such a dupe.

All very well to have a cheap land grant, but without convict labour to work it, he was on his own.

In fact, he'd be on a boat on his way back to England in an instant, could he only afford the passage.

Everything was wrong here.

The sky too blue, the sun too hot, too many bugs - half of which can kill you.

Too many jumping creatures that move too fast and will break your bones as soon as look at you.

Good eating, though, if you can catch them.

Which is hard because they move too fast and are well used to evasion.

Not enough water, not enough tea, not enough booze, not enough women.

Too many aborigines that either nick your stuff or try to kill you.

Or both.

It was definitely a mistake to come to Australia, even more, to come out here into the bush alone.

But this was his land now, and if he didn't work it, he'd lose it and be left with nothing.

Not even his dignity.

Though right at that moment, Tom wasn't sure his dignity was worth the price.

He could pretty much kiss Mary goodbye.

One or both of them would be dead before he'd established himself sufficiently to ask her to leave London for him.

The last letter he'd received was dated three months ago, and she still seemed keen when she wrote it.

But her parents were keener to get her out of the house; they'd probably sent her into service by now.

Or married her off to John the farrier.

What was wrong with him?

Why did everything he touch turn to shit?

Failed clerk that he was, why, in God's name, did he leave his nice comfortable home in search of adventure?

And why Australia of all places?

Why not America?

Or Canada?

Some other country with a thin edge of civilisation.

Not enough raw wild adventure probably.

Being a bit yellow, New Zealand had been out of the question, but relationships with the Australian aboriginals had definitely been more warlike than he'd imagined.

Tom sighed again.

The one thing to be said for working hard all day was you slept well.

No matter the surface you slept on.

He dusted up the ground a little with his booted foot before rolling out his swag.

Tom wasn't on the track anymore, so he didn't *need* to wrap all his things up in a swag, but he liked to pack it up to keep the bugs out and all his things neat and together.

In this crazy time, you never knew when you'd need to do a runner, whether for the natives, bushrangers, escaped convicts or creatures.

It easier if everything was packed and ready to go, you didn't have to risk sneaking back later to round up your stuff.

He didn't really want to take his boots off for fear of what might move into them, but they needed to air out, as did his feet.

When he put his spares on in the morning, he'd investigate them thoroughly with a stick before they got anywhere near his feet.

He lay on top of the folded blue woollen blanket, protected from the ground by a thick calico base sheet, and rested his head on the lumpy pillowcase containing his spare clothes.

The fire was dying down, sinking into itself as if it too was ashamed of consuming the trees.

Lying on his back, Tom imagined climbing its smoke to heaven, away from this hell.

He was just drifting off to sleep when he thought he heard a scream from the bush, somewhere nearby.

Sleepy and momentarily startled, his first thought was that it was just the start of another nightmare.

Nothing different tonight to any other; no reason to stress, no reason to wake up, no reason to do anything.

But then he heard it again.

He lay, eyes closed, all attention focused on the sounds he was picking up, listening intently for the scream to come again.

Was it real?

Was it a person?

Was it some kind of creature?

Out here, it could be hard to tell.

Possums hissed and snarled at night, but not like that.

And wombats grunted and squealed, but not like that.

This was a noise he hadn't noticed before.

Mind you, if he hadn't visited what passed for the local town a couple of days ago, and caught up with *The Argus* newspaper, he wouldn't have given it a second thought.

He'd have assumed it was some kind of bird or animal and ignored it.

Just rolled over and gone back to sleep.

Or what passes for sleep on stifling hot Summer nights.

But he'd got two newspaper stories stuck in his head and hadn't been able to shake them.

Two stories so typical of life in the colonies.

In the first, Mrs Stevenson had wandered into the bush and disappeared without a trace.

The marriage was rumoured to be an unhappy one. Stevenson was known to be a little too fond of a drink, and some speculated he'd killed his wife.

Perhaps because the alternatives were horrifying.

A gently treated woman alone in the bush, without food or water.

Lost on a hot day, sweating like a pig, walking or running as you looked for a way out, you'd pass out in a matter of hours.

And if you weren't found quickly, you'd probably be dead in a day.

Mind you, it wasn't exactly uncommon for outlying homesteads to be attacked by aborigines or opportunists, and human decency only got a woman alone so far.

As the scream came again, it wasn't hard to imagine some girl or young woman, lost and alone in the bush in her long white nightgown.

Screaming, waiting and listening for some kind of response before screaming again.

Though you had to ask yourself what kind of woman wonders off barefoot in her nightclothes, and whether perhaps she didn't ought to be lost in the bush and die.

Then again, some of them genteel ladies never really got to grips with life in Australia, such as it was.

Some of them were a little more fond of the laudanum bottle than was perhaps proper.

And in their drug-addled states, some of them did some stupid things.

Not that it was any of his business mind, but more a matter for her husband and the priest.

Maybe that was Mrs Stevenson's fate.

The other newspaper story was about some Simms fellow who'd got it in his head that he'd heard a lost child in the bush.

Despite no reports of missing children, they'd got up a search party and searched for days, finding no sign of the child.

The search had been called off, but that guy, haunted by some demon of his own, just wouldn't give up.

He continued searching alone; for days and days and days.

When his horse limped home alone, they went looking for him and found him dead of exhaustion.

The bush'll do that to you.

Turn you around and around, and inside out, and before you know it, you don't know where you are.

Next to no moss on the trees or otherwise to guide you home.

Not that he knew what to look for.

Life in the mean streets of a city does not prepare you adequately for bush life.

The newspapers are full of stories of men getting drunk and getting lost on their way home.

Falling over, passing out, dying of exhaustion.

Let alone those lost explorers dying of exposure after they've already eaten their horses.

Tom heard another scream, maybe a little further away this time.

If it was a woman, why didn't she call "help" or use some other words that would readily identify her as a human in danger?

The desire to be a local hero, lauded in the papers for saving some rich man's wife, warred with the risk of becoming a laughing stock like Simms.

There was a lot of free beer tied up with being a local hero, and not many would say no to that.

Certainly not Tom.

He sat up, scrubbing his eyes, trying to wake up and apply some logic to the situation before he did anything rash.

His grant was 30-acres.

He was surrounded by three other 30-acre grants.

It was about an hour's to ride to his closest neighbour, so it would take about three hours for someone to walk from his nearest neighbour to him.

Perhaps more for a woman on account of her shorter legs.

Maybe an extra hour for a child.

Assuming they followed the road, such as it was, rather than trying to cut through the bush.

And seeing as two of the grants were more or less fenced, there wasn't much point walking through the bush from them.

He only had one neighbour with a wife, and they had a child as well, though Martin was on the unfenced side.

He was good friends with Martin, so he didn't think Martin would hesitate to come ask him for help with the search.

Because two or more people are going to make a more thorough search than one.

Or at least asking you to turn up at their place in the early morning light to get a good start.

And you see more in the day than the night.

Assuming Martin had noticed he'd lost his wife or daughter at this point.

For that matter, why would Mrs Martin walk cross-country to him anyway?

Surely if they needed his help for some kind of emergency, she'd ride over, not walk.

Tom had no idea where the next closest woman or child was.

Logic suggested the scream was some kind of nocturnal wildlife he'd only noticed because he was on edge about the news articles.

He wriggled around to free the blanket from underneath him and pulled it up to his shoulder as he rolled onto his side.

It was too dark, and the terrain too rough to start looking for a woman who may or may not be lost right now.

But first thing in the morning, he'd ride over to Martin's cottage to be sure.

Hopefully that would be one more strange bush noise he could ignore in the future.

THE END

ABOUT THE AUTHOR

Alexandria Blaelock writes stories, some of them for *Ellery Queen's Mystery Magazine* and *Pulphouse Fiction Magazine*. She's also written five self-help books applying business techniques to personal matters like getting dressed, cleaning house, and feeding your friends.

As a recovering Project Manager, she's probably too fond of sticking to plan. She lives in a forest because she enjoys birdsong, the scent of gum leaves and the sun on her face. When not telecommuting to parallel universes from her Melbourne based imagination, she watches K-dramas, talks to animals, and drinks Campari. At the same time.

Discover more at www.alexandriablaelock.com.

BOOKS BY
ALEXANDRIA BLAELOCK

SHORT STORY COLLECTIONS

The Histories of Hayward Hall
Lovelorn, Lovestruck and Love at First Sight
Common or Garden Variety Heroes
Case Files of the Wilkinson Detective Agency
Unavoidable Fates
Christmas Travesties
Five Faces of Felicia Clarke

OTHER FICTION

That Love Nonsense

MS BLAELOCK'S BOOKS

Stress Free Dinner Parties
Signature Wardrobe Planning
Holistic Personal Finance
Minimally Viable Housekeeping
Planning a Life Worth Living

SHORT STORIES

Alma's Grace
Balancing the Book
Best Friends Forever
Christmas Bonanza
Christmas Business
Christmas Conflagration
Christmas Kisses
Fate in Your Hands
Lady of the Looking Glass
Life in the Security Directorate
Long Weekend in the Snow
Love in the Security Directorate
Love in the Past Tense
Morning Star, Evening Star, Superstar
Mystery of the Master Suite
Needy Bitch
Payton's Run
Phoenix Child
Remains of Christmas
Secret Singer
Shining Star
Ship in a Bottle

Simone Says Hands in the Air
Special Relativity in Space
The Bygone Boyfriend
The Day the Schedule Broke
The Ghost Detectors
The Guardian's Vigil
The Kiss of Death
The Life and Death of Carmelita Basingstoke
The Mince Pie Mystery
The Palace Hotel
The Pseudonym's Bride
The Shadow Thieves
The Space Time Paradox
Toy Soldiers
Waylon's Way

www.ingramcontent.com/pod-product-compliance
Lightning Source LLC
Chambersburg PA
CBHW030815190726
48285CB00003B/1192